The SATURDAY TRIPLETS in
Lost in the Leaf Pile

The **SATURDAY TRIPLETS** in
Lost in the Leaf Pile

by Katharine Kenah
Illustrated by Tammie Lyon

SCHOLASTIC INC.

For Rafi and Rayhan, with much love
—K.K.

For Irelyn and her supercute pic in the leaf pile—it will always be my favorite
—T.L.

ISBN 978-0-545-48143-4

Text copyright © 2013 by Katharine Kenah.
Illustrations copyright © 2013 by Tammie Lyon.
All rights reserved. Published by Scholastic Inc.
SCHOLASTIC and associated logos are trademarks and/or registered trademarks of Scholastic Inc.

12 11 10 9 8 7 6 5 4 3 2 1   13 14 15 16 17 18/0

Printed in the U.S.A.   40
First printing, September 2013
Designed by Jennifer Rinaldi Windau

It was Saturday morning.
The triplets were eating breakfast.

"Let's do something,"
said Ana.

"Something fun," said Carlos.
"I know," said Bella. "Let's rake leaves!"

"Let's go outside!" said Ana.

Their cat, Boo, followed them
out the door.

"I'll rake the fastest!" said Ana.
"I'll rake the most!" said Bella.
"I'll rake our leaves into a big pile,"
said Carlos.

Boo watched Ana rake fast.
Boo watched Bella rake the most.
Boo watched Carlos rake the leaves
into a big pile.

Bella said, "It's the biggest
leaf pile ever!"

Carlos asked, "Where is Boo?"

"He watched me rake fast,"
said Ana.

"He watched me rake the most," said Bella.
"He watched me rake our leaves into a pile," said Carlos.

"Oh, no," cried Bella.
"Maybe Boo is lost in the leaf pile!"

Ana, Bella, and Carlos
jumped into the pile.
They tossed the leaves
everywhere.

But they did
not find Boo.

The triplets were tired.
They lay down on the ground
and looked up at the sky.

Carlos's eyes opened wide.
"There's Boo!" he shouted.

"Come down, Boo!"
called Ana, Bella, and Carlos.
They hugged their cat
when he touched the ground.

The triplets raked
the biggest leaf pile ever . . .
all over again.

This time Boo was safe inside.